D1630270

BEAR in the
BIG BLUE HOUSE ™

Love Is All You Need

by Catherine Daly

based on a teleplay by Mitchell Kriegman

illustrated by Kathryn Mitter

POCKET
BOOKS

New York   London   Toronto   Sydney   Singapore

Bear sat in the living room of the Big Blue House, swinging on the bear swing with his little friend Tutter.

"Hey, you know who I was thinking about?" Bear said to Tutter. "Luna the moon! I really miss Luna and I can't wait to see her tonight. Tutter, have you ever found yourself missing someone you really love?"

"Sometimes I miss my Grandma Flutter," Tutter said. Then he thought for a moment. "Bear, what is love?" he asked.

Bear smiled. "Love is the biggest feeling inside you. It's a feeling that's warm and deep that says you really care."

"Like the way I feel when I eat cheese?" asked Tutter.

"That's right, Tutter," said Bear. "Cheese is one thing that you can love. You can love all kinds of things!"

"I do!" said Tutter. "I also love sandwiches! Especially cheese sandwiches!"

"You know, Tutter," said Bear, "everyone in the Big Blue House loves something.
You love cheese sandwiches, I love berries . . .

Ojo loves Snowbear . . .

Treelo loves feathers . . .

and Pip and Pop love clams!"

"And don't forget, you can also love your family and friends!" said Bear.

"I know, Bear! I know!" said Tutter. "I love my Grandma Flutter, and my Auntie Zipper Tutter, and my Uncle Nutter Tutter, and my cousin Klutter."

"That's a lot of Tutters to love!" said Bear.

"Oh! Oh! I almost forgot my cousins Skitter and Baby Blotter. Yes, yes, Bear, I love them too!" Tutter added.

"And do you know what else, Bear?" asked Tutter.

"What?" asked Bear.

"I love you too!" Tutter gave Bear a big hug. Then he jumped down from the swing and ran off to find Ojo. They were going to play with her toy aeroplane. Tutter couldn't wait. He *loved* toy aeroplanes.

Just then Pip and Pop appeared. "Did somebody say love?" they asked together.

"Oh, hi," said Bear. "I was just talking to Tutter about love and –"

"Bear, we *love* love!" Pip and Pop interrupted.

The truth was, Pip and Pop loved everything! They loved Bear's swing, they loved the living-room table, they loved the pillows on the couch and, most of all, they loved Bear.

"But does Bear love us?" they asked worriedly. "Do you Bear? Do you? Huh?"

"Yes!" Bear exclaimed. "Of course! I love you guys! You're the best!"

Pip and Pop looked at each other. "But how much do you love us, Bear?"

"Hmm," said Bear thoughtfully. "My love for you is bigger than the couch!"

"Whoa!" said Pip and Pop. "That's a lot of love! But our love is even bigger! It's bigger than the whole living room!"

Bear was impressed. That was pretty big! But then he had an idea. "My love is bigger than all the berries I've ever eaten!" he said.

"Whoa!" said Pip and Pop. "That's a lot of berries!"

Pip shook his head. "What could be bigger than that?" he asked.

"We'll have to think about it and get back to you," said Pop.

"See you later, Bear!" Pip said.

"Well, where was I?" said Bear. "Oh, that's right! I was thinking about my friend Luna and how I can't wait to see her!"

Just then Bear was interrupted by a loud noise. Someone was yelling. It was coming from the kitchen. It sounded like Ojo!

Bear walked into the kitchen. Next to Ojo on the floor was a broken wooden aeroplane.
"That's it!" Ojo said to Tutter. "I'm never letting you play with anything of mine again!"
"But Ojo," said Tutter. "I didn't mean to break it!"

Ojo was angry. "Tutter, I don't want to be your friend any more," she said.

Tutter gasped. "Well! Well!" he spluttered. "I don't want to be *your* friend either. So there!"

Bear tried to help out. "You know, just because you have a disagreement doesn't mean that . . ."

But before Bear could finish his sentence, Ojo stormed out of the kitchen and Tutter went back into his mouse hole.

Bear headed over to the otter pond, where he found Ojo.

"Can you believe it, Bear?" said Ojo. "He broke my favourite plane! That Tutter!"

"I don't think he . . ." began Bear.

"I know, I know, Bear – Tutter didn't mean it! But my aeroplane is broken!" Ojo complained.

Bear told Ojo he could probably fix the broken aeroplane with some glue. "Wow! That would be great!" said Ojo. "But I'm not saying I'm sorry to Tutter! No way! I can play just fine by myself."

Bear returned to the kitchen and got down to work.

Tutter came out of his mouse hole and found Bear gluing the plane back together. "Is that Ojo's aeroplane?" Tutter asked with a gasp.

"I thought I'd just try to mend it," said Bear.

Tutter frowned. "Well, don't look at me, Bear. It wasn't my fault! I tell you, it wasn't my fault!"

Bear didn't say anything. Tutter continued. "I know Ojo didn't mean to yell at me," he said. "But she did! There's no way I'm saying I'm sorry. No way!"

Bear shook his head sadly. He hoped that Tutter and Ojo would make up soon.

A little while later, Bear went back to the kitchen to inspect the aeroplane. The glue was dry. Ojo's aeroplane looked almost as good as new!

Just then Ojo and Tutter walked into the kitchen.

"Hi, guys!" said Bear.

But Ojo and Tutter didn't even notice Bear. They were so happy to see each other! "I'm sorry!" they said together.

Ojo pointed to the aeroplane.

"Hey look, Tutter!" she shouted. "My aeroplane's fixed!"

"Now we can fly to Ojo Island!" said Tutter.

Ojo picked up the aeroplane, and they started to head out of the kitchen.

Bear was surprised. "Wait a second!" he said. "What just happened?"

Tutter and Ojo explained that since they were such good friends, they couldn't stay cross with each other for long.

"That's because you *love* each other!" said Bear happily.

Tutter and Ojo ran off to the living room to play. Bear started tidying the kitchen, whistling happily to himself. Suddenly he had an idea. He grabbed the glue, some glitter, some colourful paper and some other things, and called Tutter, Ojo, Pip, Pop and Treelo into the kitchen.

"I have an idea!" Bear exclaimed. "Since the Big Blue House is filled with so much love today, let's make special cards for each other!"

Everyone thought that sounded like a lot of fun! They all started cutting, pasting and colouring.

Soon it was time to hand out the cards. Tutter made one for Ojo. It had a picture of Snowbear on it. And Ojo made a card with a big piece of cheese on it for Tutter.

Pip and Pop made Treelo a card with a beautiful feather glued on to it. And Treelo's card for Pip and Pop had a picture of a big pile of clams on it!

Bear made special cards for everyone.
"What do your cards to us say, Bear?" asked Tutter.
Bear smiled. "They say, 'Roses are red, and so are cherries. I love you as much as I love berries! Love, Bear.'"

Then Tutter handed Bear the bear-sized card they had all made together.

"Hey, Bear," said Pip and Pop, "we love you as much as – all the clams in the ocean!"

"And I love you as much as I love Snowbear," said Ojo.

"And I love you as much as cheese sandwiches!" said Tutter.

"Feathers!" said Treelo.

"Wow!" said Bear. "I don't think I can do better than that!" He smiled. "But let me just say that I love you all enough to give you a big old Bear hug!"

That night, Bear told Luna all about the fight that Ojo and Tutter had, and how they made up. He told her about how everyone made cards for each other. And he also told her about how he missed her all day.

"Well, Bear, you know that even when I'm not around, I'm always thinking of you," Luna said.

"Oh, Luna, I love you," said Bear.

"I love you, too, Bear," said Luna.